To Leighton and Luke:
May you always keep your eyes open for a friend in need of a little help
NW

To James and his crew of fun friends
CT

The illustrations in this book were watercolored in Windsor and Newton paint on Strathmore paper.
The text was set in Canterbury-Regular.

ISBN: 978-0-578-88590-2

Printed in China

www.nataliewellsfry.com

A key to success is sometimes asking
for help. Look for keys hiding around
the helpful friends in this book.

hi! I'm ladybug.
Look for me on every page!

COCK-A-DOODLE-DOO!

DO I KNOW YOU?

written by
NATALIE WELLSFRY

illustrated by
CLAIRE THOMPSON

PRONUNCIATIONS

Cock-a-doodle-doo
(English)

Chicchirichì
Italian
(ki-ki-re-kee)

Koke-kokko
Japanese
(ko-ke-ko-ko)

Cocorico
French
(co-co-re-co)

Scan me to hear how roosters
sound around the world!

COCK-A-DOODLE-DOO!

Do I know you?

You look just like my old friend, Hugh!

KI-KI-RE-KEE!

I don't know how that could be!
I'm Roo, the new kid here from Italy.

But if it's Hugh you're looking for, and Hugh looks like me,
let's go look for him together! How fun would that be?!

Thank you, Roo, for helping with my search!
I know just who to ask! He lives right past that church.

His name is Ollie Owl and he knows everything, you see.
Come along and meet him! I know you will agree!

COCK-A-DOODLE-DOO!

KI-KI-RE-KEE!

Ollie are you free?
It's Willie, please come down from your tree!

Here's my new friend Roo, and we're out looking for Hugh. If anyone knows where to find him, surely it's you!

HOOT HOOT!

Hiya there you two! I hope I can be
of aid. A rooster moved to Farm Lane,
but I don't know his name I'm afraid.

And Roo, he sounds a lot like you, and looks like you both a ton,
but his call's a little different when he wakes us with the sun.

Is it you we're looking for?

Ollie sent us over, but I've never seen you before.

Oh how silly I am to think it'd be this easy.

I thought we'd find Hugh easy peezy lemon squeezy.

Maybe I was wrong and should give up now and quit.

The world is so very large, I don't know half of it!

KO-KE-KO-KO!

No siree, Hugh is not me. I moved here from
Japan, but I'll help and that makes three!
With all of us together, I know we'll find your friend.
Don't give up! We can do it! He'll turn up in the end.

And although I'm not your buddy, I think you will find out,
the journey can be tough but it's what life is all about.

SQUEAK SQUEAK!

Excuse me you three, I'm sorry to chime in.

I couldn't help but overhear the pickle that you're in.

Please don't stop your searching, and don't feel quite so sad.
I know that you'll find him! There's more fun to be had!
Sometimes when I feel blue and don't know what
to do, I like to go somewhere new and get
a different view.

It's awesome what you can see from here!
Wow, what a show! And there off past
that meadow, I see another town!
Let's all go over to it and have a look around.

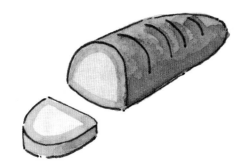
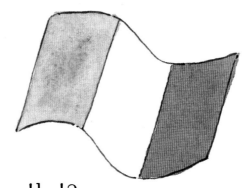

Listen! Do you hear that?
A rooster that sounds like Hugh!
He's French, did I tell you?
I forgot... that was my clue!

And now that I think of it,
how fun it is to know,
none of us are the same

BUT IN OUR DIFFERENCES WE GROW.

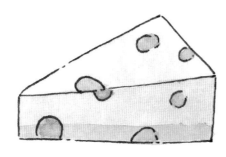

CO-CO-RE-CO!

Willie! What a wonderful surprise!
It's been so very long.
I cannot believe my eyes!

Hugh! I'm so glad we found you! I thought we never would.
But my new friends never doubted, they always knew we could.

What a special day. I didn't just find my friend...

I made more friends along the way. Oh what a happy end!